MW00955229

To Marcy - My new first love. _

www.mascotbooks.com

Are You My Motherboard?

For more information, please contact:
Mascot Books
620 Herndon Parkway, Suite 320
Herndon, VA 20170
info@mascotbooks.com

Library of Congress Control Number: 2017916111

CPSIA Code: PRT1117A
ISBN-13: 978-1-68401-519-1

Printed in the United States

ARE YOU MY MOTHERBOARD?_

Dr. Chris Masullo

Illustrated by Kayla Dailey & Joseph Dziema

Arty had been doing his chores and helping his neighbors, saving every penny he earned.

Tomorrow was going to be a very special day because he had finally saved enough money to buy the computer parts he needed. _

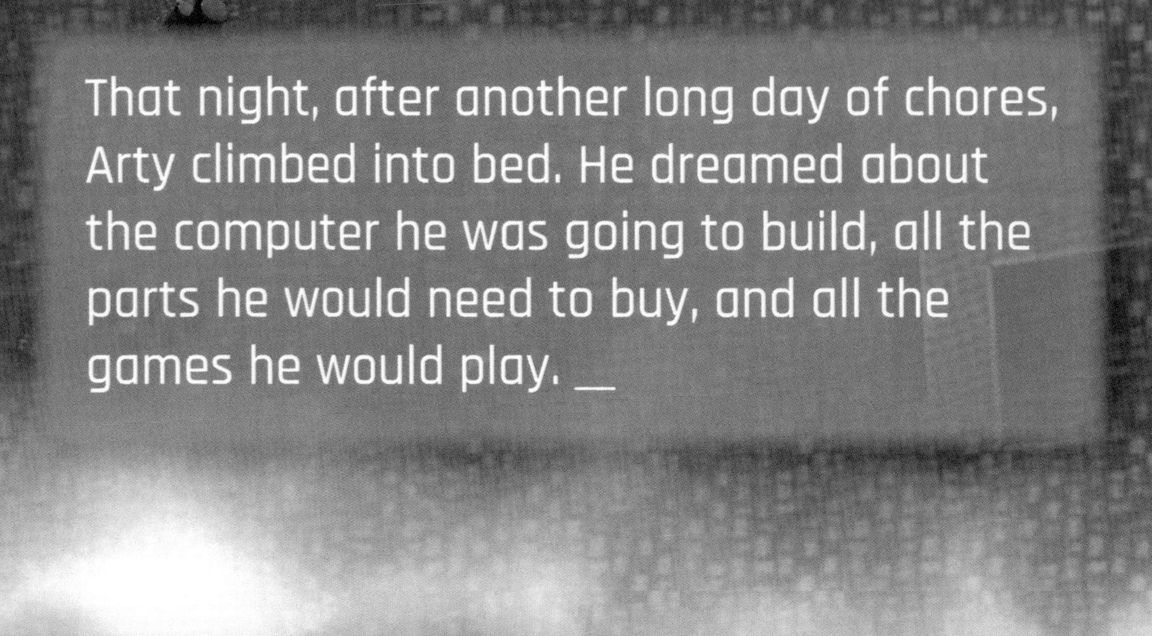
That night, after another long day of chores, Arty climbed into bed. He dreamed about the computer he was going to build, all the parts he would need to buy, and all the games he would play. _

Arty slipped into his cyberspace dream world—a land of technology and wonderment where his dream of building a computer could become a reality.

He knew enough about computers to know that the motherboard was the most important part of the computer because all of the other parts needed to connect to it. _

Travelling along the information superhighway, Arty stumbled upon his first computer part. **"Are you my motherboard?"** he asked. _

"No," the big black box replied. "I am a computer case. I can lay flat on your desk or stand tall like a tower. It's my job to keep all the parts of the computer safe, just like your skeleton keeps all of your organs safe. I also keep unwanted objects out, just like your skin."

Arty recognized the importance of the case and so he asked it to join him on his journey. _

Soon, Arty and the case were greeted by another computer component. This one had wires sticking out of its top like a moppy head of hair.
"Are you my motherboard?" Arty asked eagerly.

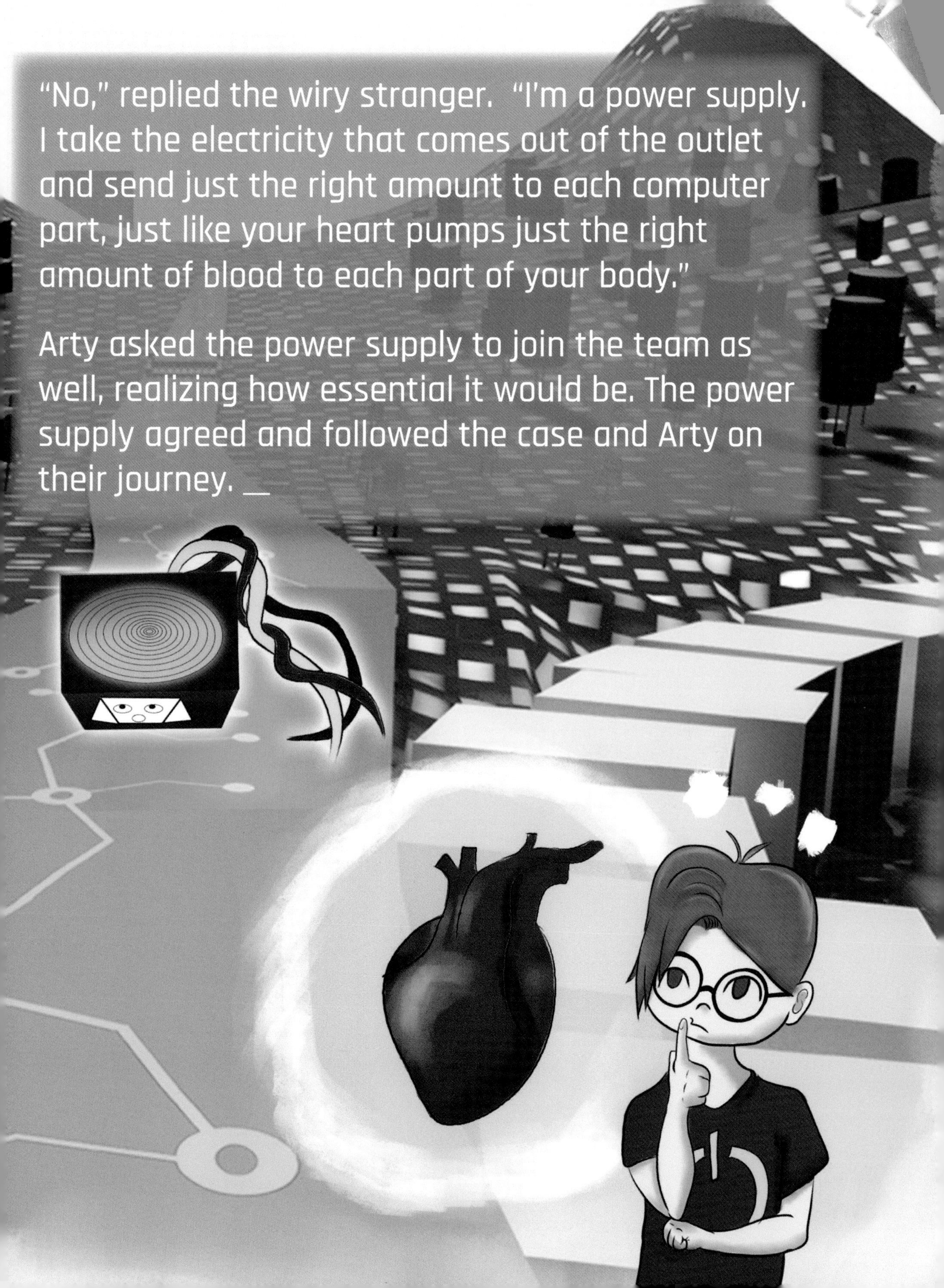

"No," replied the wiry stranger. "I'm a power supply. I take the electricity that comes out of the outlet and send just the right amount to each computer part, just like your heart pumps just the right amount of blood to each part of your body."

Arty asked the power supply to join the team as well, realizing how essential it would be. The power supply agreed and followed the case and Arty on their journey.

Before they knew it, the team crossed paths with another computer component.

"Are you my motherboard?" Arty asked hopefully.

"No," replied the skinny circuit. "I'm the memory. My nickname is 'RAM'—it stands for 'Random Access Memory.' I'm the place where computers store information for short periods of time while it's still needed. Later, that information gets erased, just like your short term memory does when you sleep."

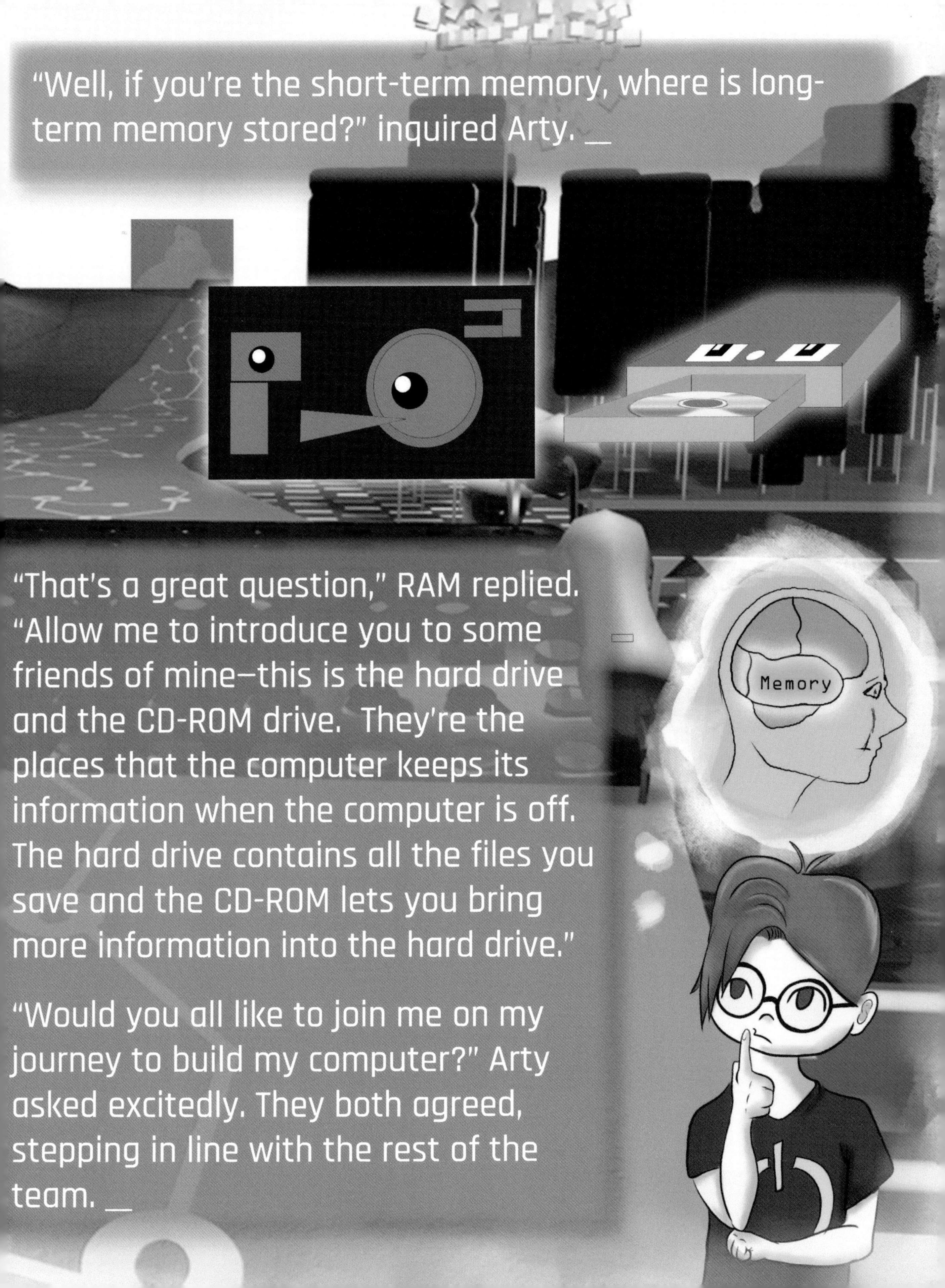

"Well, if you're the short-term memory, where is long-term memory stored?" inquired Arty. _

"That's a great question," RAM replied. "Allow me to introduce you to some friends of mine—this is the hard drive and the CD-ROM drive. They're the places that the computer keeps its information when the computer is off. The hard drive contains all the files you save and the CD-ROM lets you bring more information into the hard drive."

"Would you all like to join me on my journey to build my computer?" Arty asked excitedly. They both agreed, stepping in line with the rest of the team. _

Arty and his new friends continued down the windy road until they met a shiny little square with a big top hat.

"Are you my motherboard?" Arty asked.

"No, I'm the central processing unit—'CPU' for short," it replied. "I'm the brains of the computer. I direct all of the operations from the moment you start the computer until you turn it off."

"You mean, you're in control of everything?" Arty asked with wide eyes.

"Yep!" replied the CPU. "Absolutely everything. Press a key, move the mouse—every time you play a game, surf the web, save a file, or print a picture, I'm in charge."

"You sound very important!" Arty proclaimed and asked him to join the team.

"I certainly am," the CPU responded, "but there is one more thing you will need before your journey can be completed."

"The motherboard!" everyone shouted, marching onward.

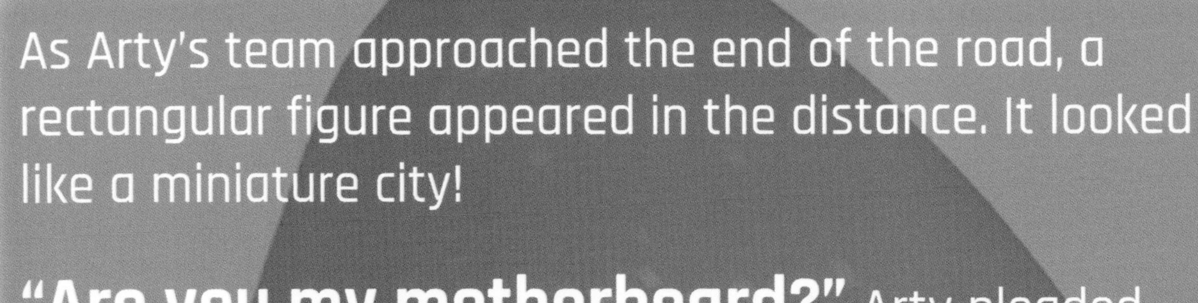

As Arty's team approached the end of the road, a rectangular figure appeared in the distance. It looked like a miniature city!

"Are you my motherboard?" Arty pleaded, one last time. _

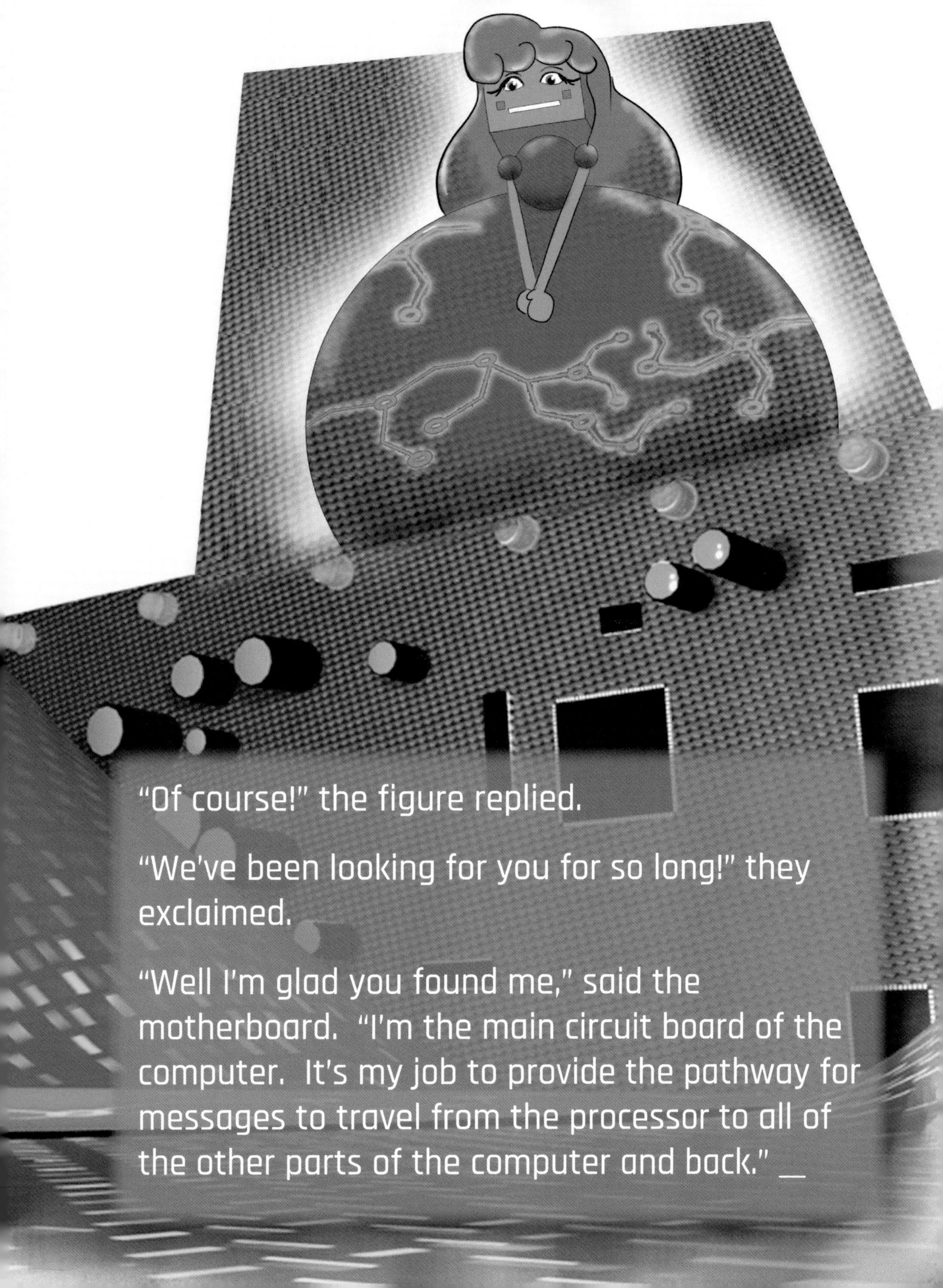

"Of course!" the figure replied.

"We've been looking for you for so long!" they exclaimed.

"Well I'm glad you found me," said the motherboard. "I'm the main circuit board of the computer. It's my job to provide the pathway for messages to travel from the processor to all of the other parts of the computer and back."

"Like how the nervous system carries messages from my brain?" asked Arty.

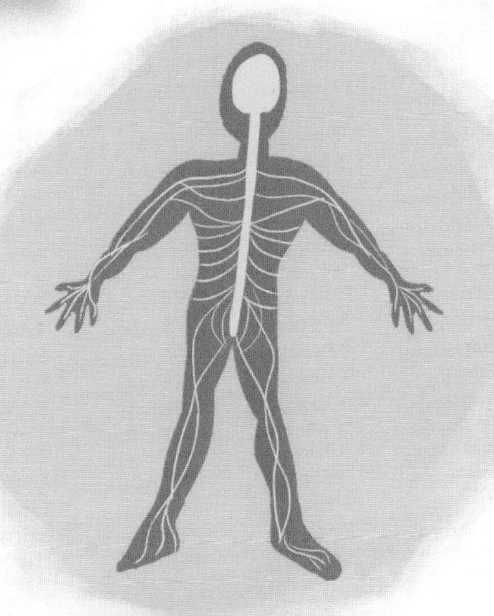

"Yes," replied the motherboard. "The processor sits on my back—the memory, too. All of the other parts connect to me in one way or another. I make sure the messages get from the processor to the hard drive to the printer, and everywhere else in-between."

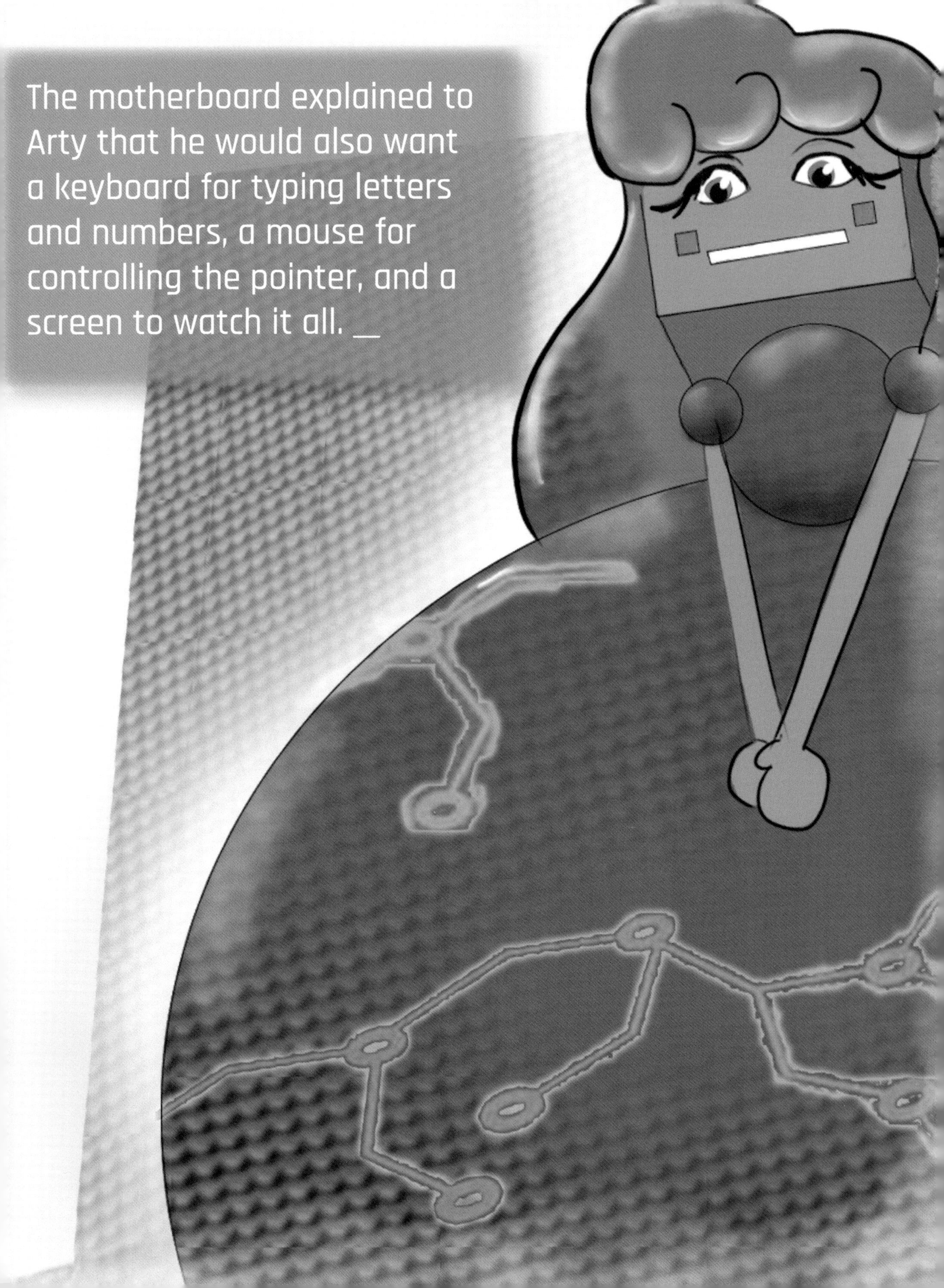
The motherboard explained to
Arty that he would also want
a keyboard for typing letters
and numbers, a mouse for
controlling the pointer, and a
screen to watch it all. _

Arty was overjoyed to finally have all the parts he would need to build his very own computer. "We come together as a team to make the whole system work!" the computer parts rejoiced.

Arty woke with a start. He looked at his clock and counted the hours until his parents would take him to the computer store. _

Fall Gaming Sale!
Fall Gaming Sale!
R.A.M
R.A.M
R.A.M
R.A.M
8GB
CPU
CJK 2000
PC Case
CJK 2000
PC Case
CJK 2000
PC Case

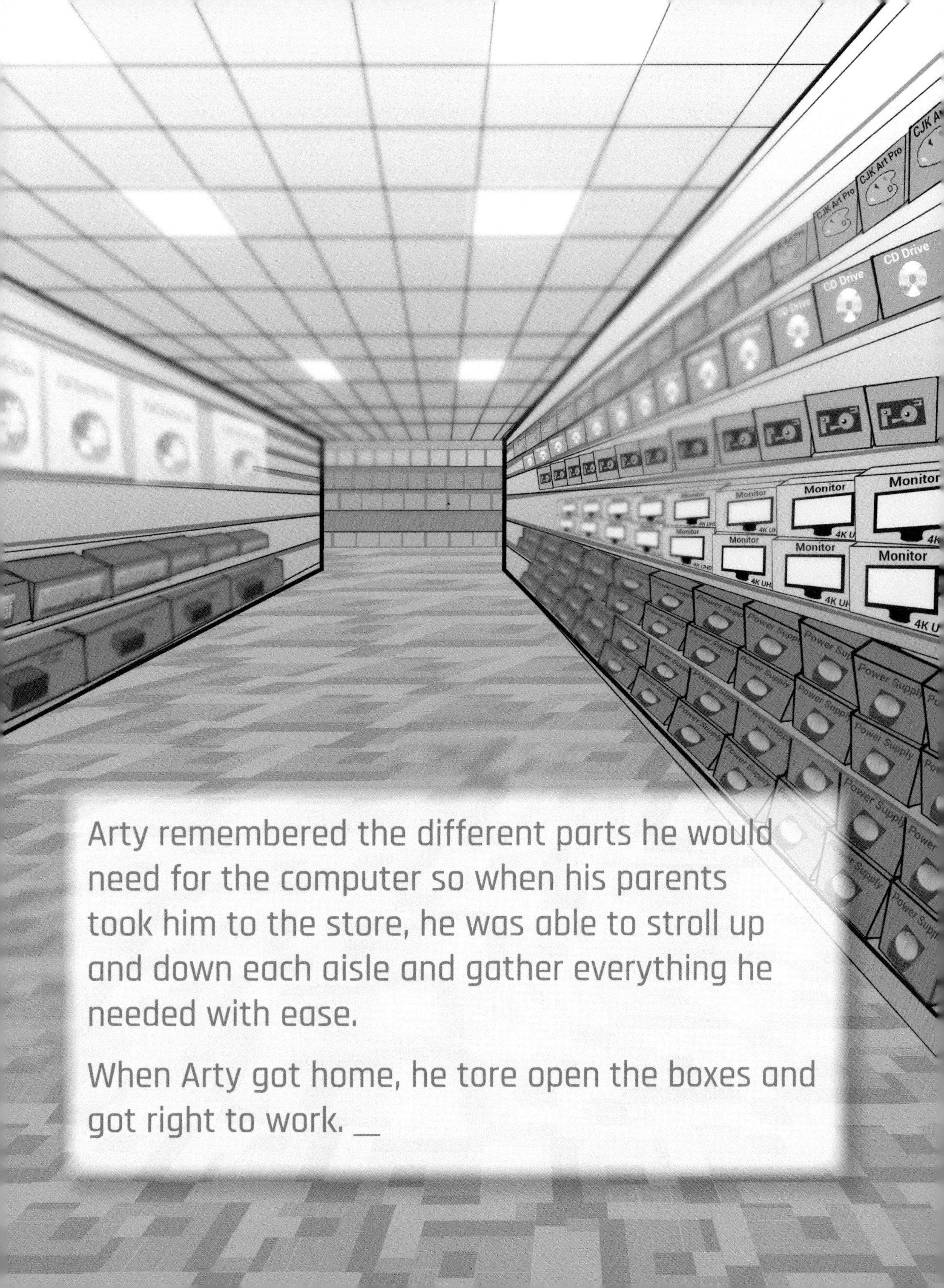

Arty remembered the different parts he would need for the computer so when his parents took him to the store, he was able to stroll up and down each aisle and gather everything he needed with ease.

When Arty got home, he tore open the boxes and got right to work. _

First, he opened the computer case and attached the power supply inside, just like Motherboard had instructed him.

Then, he clipped in the RAM and CPU to Motherboard and carefully fastened the trio inside the case.

Arty inserted the hard drive and CD-ROM drive before making the connections one by one.

He added a fan to keep the CPU cool and plugged in the keyboard, mouse, and monitor.

Finally, Arty plugged the power supply safely into a power strip.

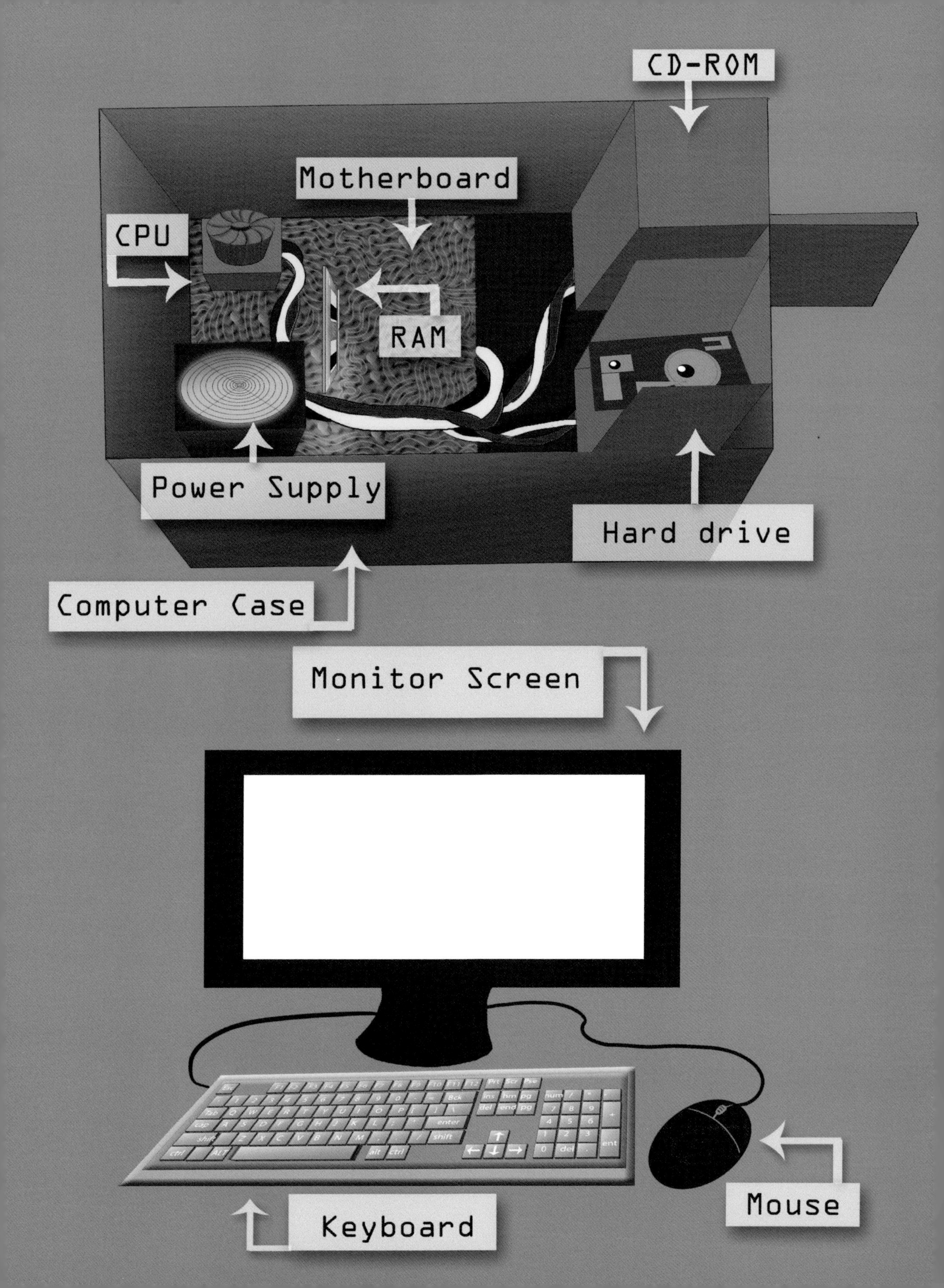

CD-ROM
Motherboard
CPU
RAM
Power Supply
Hard drive
Computer Case
Monitor Screen
Keyboard
Mouse

File Effects Undo Help
CJK Art Pro
Recover
Arty's Videos
Explore
Homework
Arty's Pics
CJK Art Pro
Games
7:00PM

The moment Arty had been waiting for had finally come. He looked with pride at the complete computer system that he built all by himself.

The computer whirred, beeped, ticked, and clicked as Arty switched it on. The lights blinked as it hummed.

"Thank you, Motherboard," he said with a smile. _

THE END_

Help Arty find the computer terms!_

Q I Y J D P O W E R S U P P L Y L U O A V X W Q

A Y U L F R I S W E R P G K F Y A L K B L S A M

W V W F Q H R B X Y T C Y S X F W R G U C W S B

G E H T D E T J U E G H U W H O P O D H B V D W

X W E T Y G I H Y T W Q D J L H R G N J K I U R

V R H Y K I O A S Q E R T Y U M O P F T G H J K

B N M J K Z W K E Y B O A R D M U I O P J H T J

B N M K L O E G F R T Y U I O O F Q W R T Y J K

L P O K H D R F R E X S A D F T H J K L J M Z A

F G J Y K L V F R T Y U I O K H D E G B W K L S

A Z X S D E F C A S E T Y U I E V I R D D R A H

S R F T R D G H A T Q E R G H R K L V C B A M J

M F N H J K R A X C V B N M T B H J L M N M K H

A O D R G G Y R T G T Q I P E O F S D F G H J W

E D U E X C V B N M T F G R G A F G H B V C V S

D F G T A Z X C V B T G E F G R R F E G H G E E

F G H N E K R F G E G H U E Q D E R T Y U G T Y

H J U I D F G H J N B V C X D F G J O L P T P A

Z X C R B N M O N I T O R T X D G H J K L Y U I

Q W S P E F R G H C D R O M T O P A S D F E F T

MOUSE
CPU
HARD DRIVE
RAM
CD ROM
MONITOR

POWER SUPPLY
CASE
MOTHERBOARD
KEYBOARD
TOWER
PRINTER

Computer Crossword

ACROSS

1. random access memory
3. screen
5. controls pointer
7. long term storage
8. powers up computer

DOWN

2. main circuit board
4. type with this
6. "brains" of the computer
9. keeps computer safe
10. compact disc read-only memory

Help Arty find Motherboard! _

ABOUT THE AUTHOR

Dr. Chris Masullo is a mathematics teacher and technology facilitator. He has taught all grade levels from pre-k through college. When computers were first introduced into the classroom back in the 5th grade, it was love at first sight for Chris. Back then, the games were on large floppy discs, monochrome, and required more imagination than anything else, but it didn't matter. Chris pursued a career in teaching and earned a doctoral degree in instructional technology, always staying close to his first love—computers. _